# DISCOVERING
# SEASHELLS

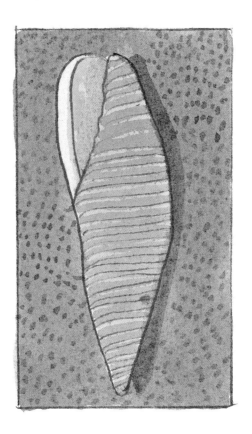

# DOUGLAS FLORIAN

CHARLES SCRIBNER'S SONS • NEW YORK

Inside every empty seashell there once lived a soft animal called a *mollusk* (mol-usk). Mollusks don't have skeletons inside their bodies as we do. Their hard shells are like outside skeletons. The shells protect them from other animals.

Some mollusks live on land, like these English Garden Snails, but most mollusks live in the sea.

This book is about sea or *marine* mollusks.

English Garden Snails

2 times life-size

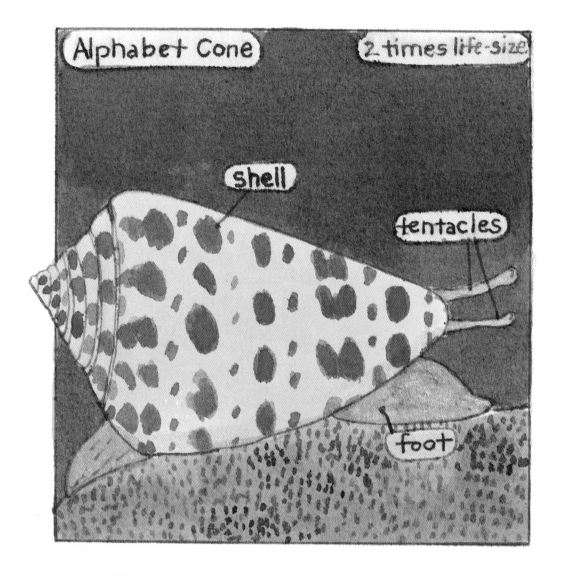

There are two major groups of mollusks. A *univalve* (*uni* means one) lives inside a single shell. It has a head with eyes, a mouth, and *tentacles*. Tentacles are like fingers that help the animal feel the world around it. Univalves also have a muscular part called a *foot*. They crawl along the ocean floor on the foot. The Alphabet Cone is a univalve found along the coast of Florida and Mexico.

The Painted Top Shell mollusk has two long tentacles on its head and smaller tentacles on its side. It lives in the North Atlantic Ocean and in the Mediterranean Sea.

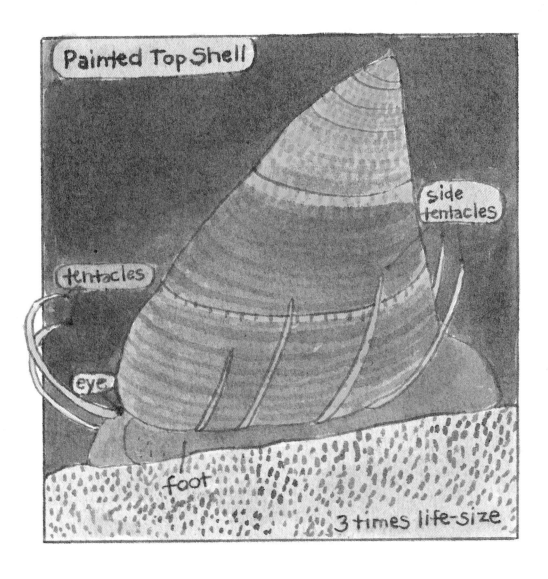

The other large group of mollusks is called *bivalves* (*bi* means two). A bivalve lives in two shells that are joined. It doesn't have a head, but it does have a foot. It also has two muscles to hold its shell closed. The Angel Wing is a bivalve. It's found along the east coast from Massachusetts to the Caribbean.

The place where a mollusk naturally lives is called its *habitat.* The habitat of the Jackknife Clam is the sandy bottom of shallow water.

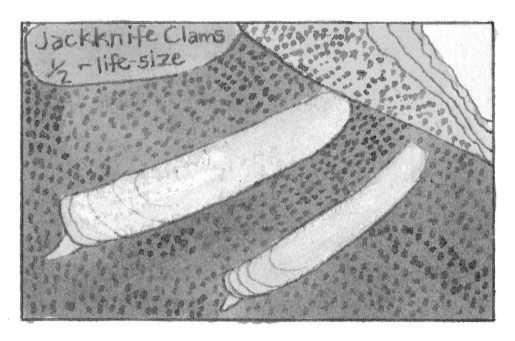

The Zebra Periwinkle lives on the rocky shore.

The Camel Cowrie's habitat is on coral reefs.

The Purple Sea Snail floats on top of the water.

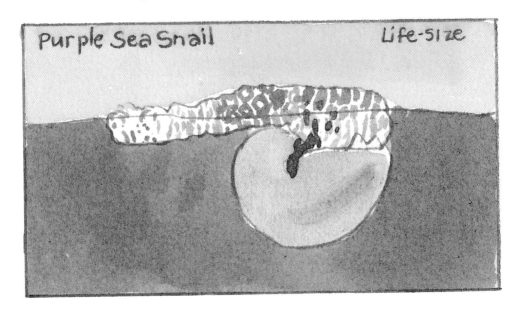

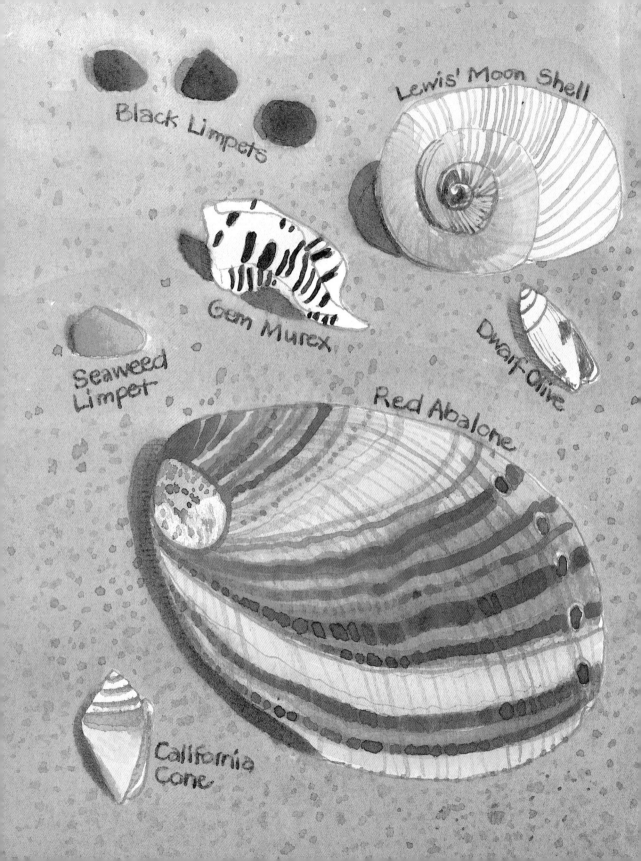

Black Limpets

Lewis' Moon Shell

Gem Murex

Dwarf Olive

Seaweed Limpet

Red Abalone

California Cone

No seashell is found in every ocean of the world. Scientists divide the oceans into eighteen parts called *provinces*. Shells of mollusks from the warmer provinces are more colorful than those from colder provinces.

The Californian Province has the warm waters of the west coast of the United States. These are some of the shells of that province.

Pacific
White Venus

Annette's Cowrie

All shells life-size

Ivory Tusk

Knobbed Whelk

The Carolinian Province has the waters of the Eastern shore, from the Carolinas to the Gulf Coast of the South. You can find these shells in the Carolinian Province.

Yellow Cockle

Flame Auger

American Pelican's Foot

Beautiful
Top Shell

Sunrise Tellin

Shells come in many different shapes.
Moon Shells and Nerites are round.

Top Shells are shaped like tops.

Tusk Shells have the long shape of an elephant's tusk.

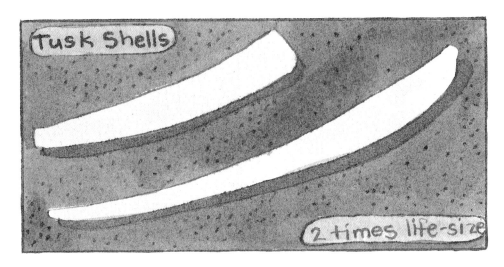

Tusk Shells

2 times life-size

Murex Shells have long sharp spines. The spines protect the mollusk from attack.

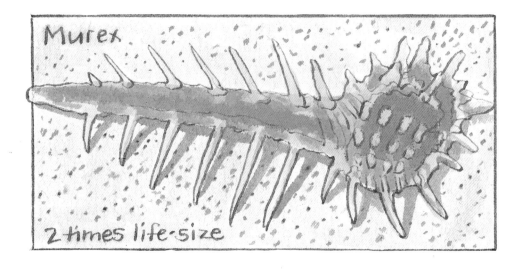

Murex

2 times life-size

The Heart Cockle gets its name from its heart shape. It lives near coral in the Pacific.

The West Indian Worm Shell is shaped much like a worm. It's found in Southern Florida and in the West Indies.

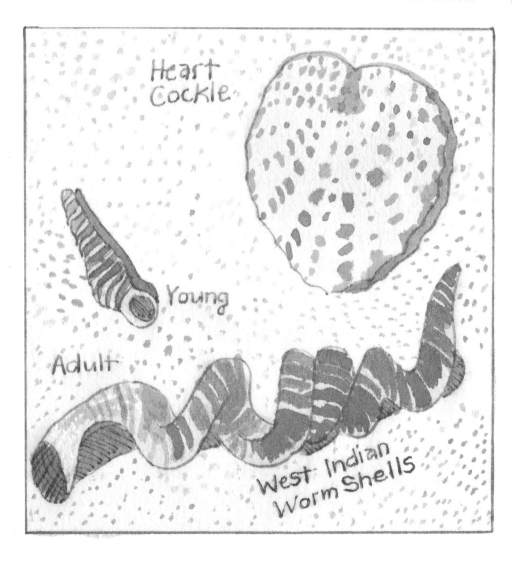

The Prince Thorny Oyster has many long white spines.
This beautiful shell is found on the west coast of the Americas
and is prized by collectors.

Seashells have been valued by people for many years. The ancient Greeks used Murex Snails to make a purple dye. Some cultures created musical instruments from shells. The *shanka* is a trumpet made in India from a Conch Shell. The *hobagai* (ho-buh-guy) is a Conch trumpet used in Japan in the seventh century.

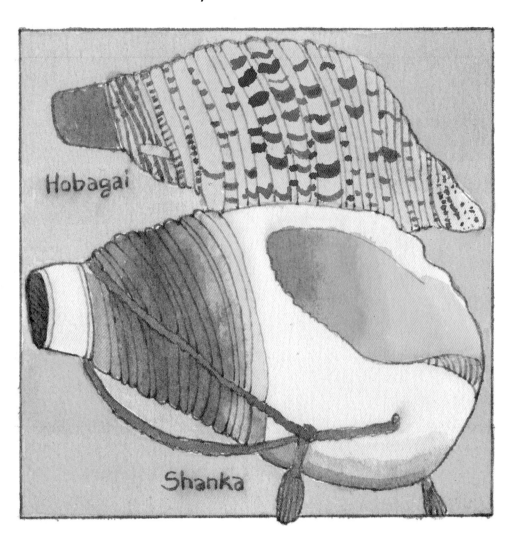

In central Africa Cowrie Shells were strung together
to make a rattle.

Shells are also valued for their great beauty.
The Textile Cone Shell is a pleasure to look at, but
the sting of its mollusk can be deadly.

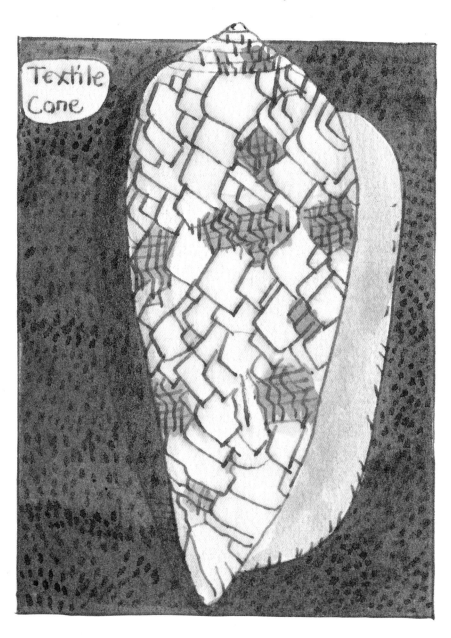

The Florida Fighting Conch and the Pink Conch are beautifully colored. Both shells are found in southern Florida.

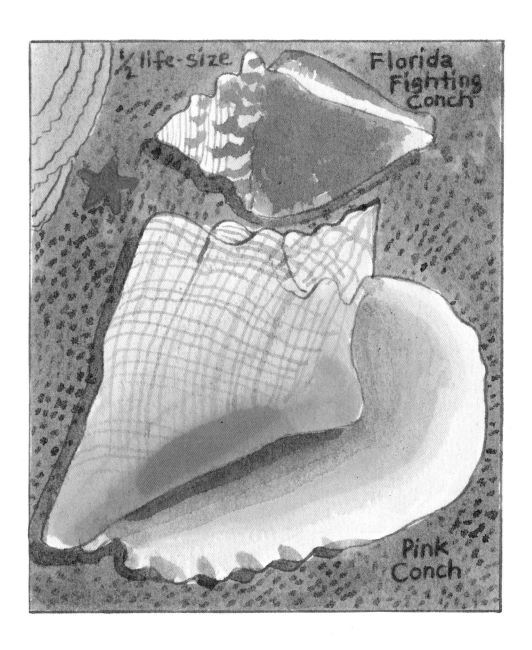

½ life-size

Florida Fighting Conch

Pink Conch

Scientists divide mollusks into *families*. One large family is the Keyhole Limpet family. In North America there are more than 100 different species, or kinds, of Keyhole Limpets. The Keyhole Limpet has a hole in the center of its shell that looks like a keyhole.

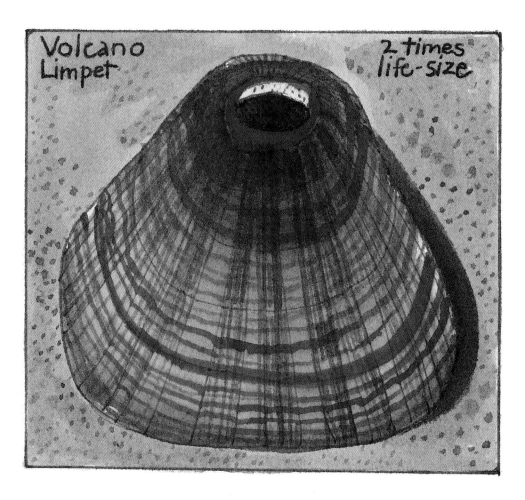

Volcano Limpet

2 times life-size

The Volcano Limpet is in this family. It looks something like a volcano with red hot lava.

Northern Yellow
Periwinkles

3 times
life-size

The Periwinkle family is also large, but the shells are small, always less than two inches. Periwinkles can live on rocky shores. The Northern Yellow Periwinkle is found along the northeast shore of the United States.

Tent Olive

Purple Dwarf Olive

The Olive Shell family is known for its beauty. Olive Shells come in many different colors and patterns. The Tent-olive Shell is covered with a geometric pattern. The Dwarf Olive is gray or purple.

The Scallop family is very common throughout the world. Scallop Shells are shaped like fans. The two triangles at the bottom are called *ears*.

The Atlantic Deepsea Scallop has a flat shell up to eight inches in length.

Atlantic Deepsea Scallop

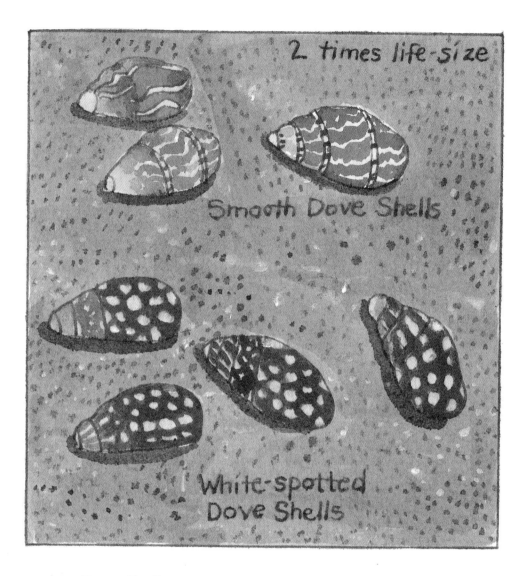

2 times life-size

Smooth Dove Shells

White-spotted
Dove Shells

Dove Shells are also very common in all the seas. Most Dove Shells are less than one inch long. The Smooth Dove Shell and the White-spotted Dove Shell are found along the southern coast of Florida.

One of the most unusual mollusk families is the Carrier Shell. These shells carry other shells and stones along with them for protection from attack. The Curly Carrier Shell is from the Mediterranean Sea.

Some shells of a family may be common while others may be rare. The Golden Cowrie of the Pacific Ocean is quite rare. But the Panther Cowrie, also from the Pacific, is very common.

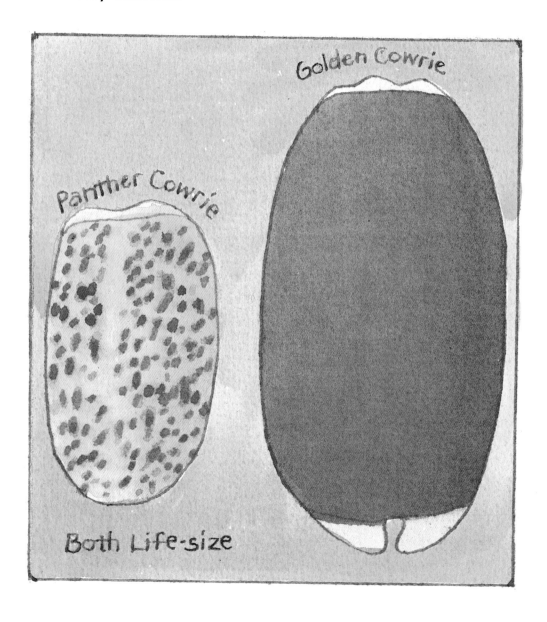

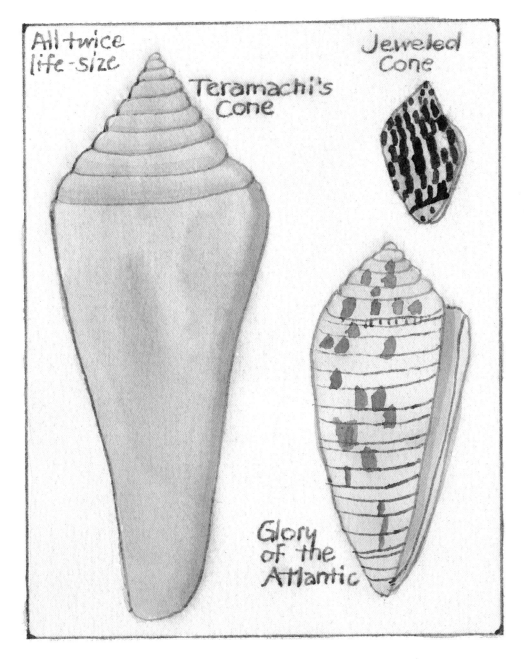

The Jeweled Cone and the Glory of the Atlantic are rare Cone Shells of the Caribbean Sea and the Florida coast. Teramachi's Cone from Japan is also rare.

Starting a seashell collection is easy, especially if you live near the ocean. On a beach you can find shells of mollusks that live in the sand as well as in shallow water. After a storm a lot of shells are washed up along the shore.

You can find shells on a rocky shore also. Here shells hide in the cracks between rocks and under rocks.

Collect your shells in a strong plastic bag or bucket. Later you can clean them with an old toothbrush and soap and water.

You can store your shells in boxes or in drawers. Some people like to label their shells with a number in ink. Then they write all the information about that shell on an index card.

# For Elena

Charles Scribner's Sons Books for Young Readers
Macmillan Publishing Company
866 Third Avenue, New York, NY 10022
Collier Macmillan Canada, Inc.

Printed in Japan by Toppan Printing Co.

10  9  8  7  6  5  4  3  2

Library of Congress Cataloging-in-Publication Data
Florian, Douglas,      Discovering seashells.
Summary: An introduction to various kinds of seashells,
where they can be found, and their early inhabitants.
1. Shells—Juvenile literature. [1. Shells] I. Title.
QL405.2.F56  1986      594'.0471      86-11903
ISBN 0-684-18740-X